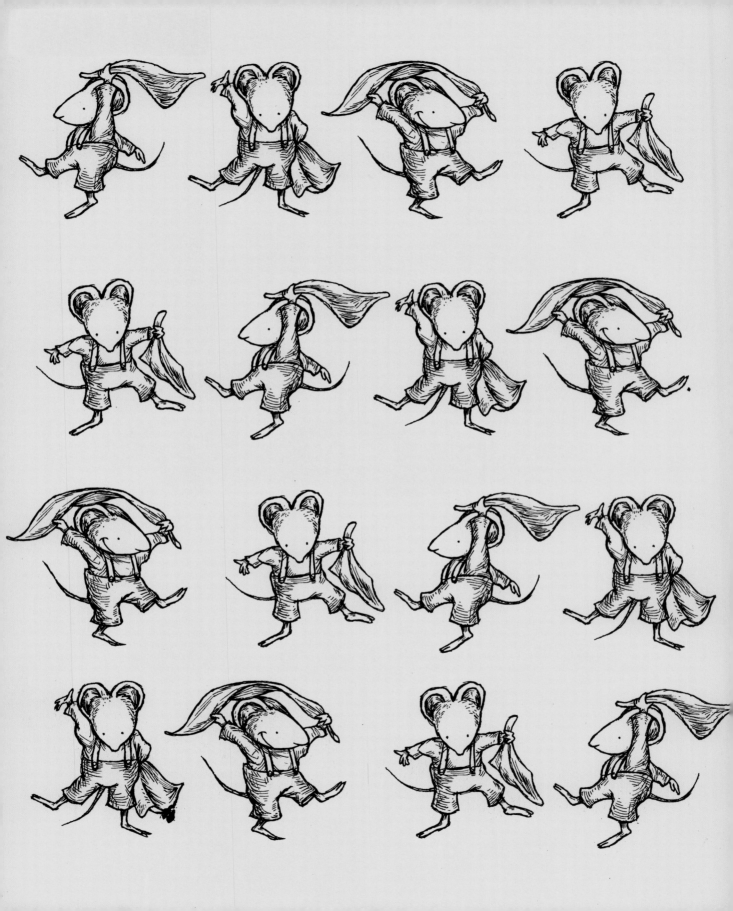

Owen

· KEVIN HENKES ·

RED FOX

FOR LAURA

A Red Fox Book

Published by Random House Children's Books
20 Vauxhall Bridge Road, London SW1V 2SA
A division of The Random House Group Ltd
London Melbourne Sydney Auckland
Johannesburg and agencies throughout the world

Copyright text and illustrations © Kevin Henkes 1993

1 3 5 7 9 10 8 6 4 2

First published in the USA by Greenwillow Books 1993
First published in Great Britain by Julia MacRae 1995
Red Fox edition 1999

Printed in Singapore

RANDOM HOUSE UK Limited Reg. No. 954009

ISBN 0 09 187304 5

Owen had a fuzzy yellow blanket.

He'd had it since he was a baby.

He loved it with all his heart.

"Fuzzy goes where I go," said Owen.

And Fuzzy did.

Upstairs, downstairs, in-between.

Inside, outside, upside down.

"Fuzzy likes what I like," said Owen.

And Fuzzy did.

Orange juice, grape juice, chocolate milk.

Ice cream, peanut butter, applesauce cake.

"Isn't he getting a little old to be carrying that thing around?" asked Mrs. Tweezers. "Haven't you heard of the Blanket Fairy?"

Owen's parents hadn't.

Mrs. Tweezers filled them in.

That night Owen's parents told Owen to put Fuzzy under
his pillow.

In the morning Fuzzy would be gone, but the Blanket Fairy
would leave an absolutely wonderful, positively perfect,
especially terrific big-boy gift in its place.

Owen stuffed Fuzzy inside his pyjama trousers
and went to sleep.

"No Blanket Fairy," said Owen in the morning.

"No kidding," said Owen's mother.

"No wonder," said Owen's father.

"Fuzzy's dirty," said Owen's mother.

"Fuzzy's torn and ratty," said Owen's father.

"No," said Owen. "Fuzzy is perfect."

And Fuzzy was.

Fuzzy played Captain Plunger with Owen.

Fuzzy helped Owen become invisible.

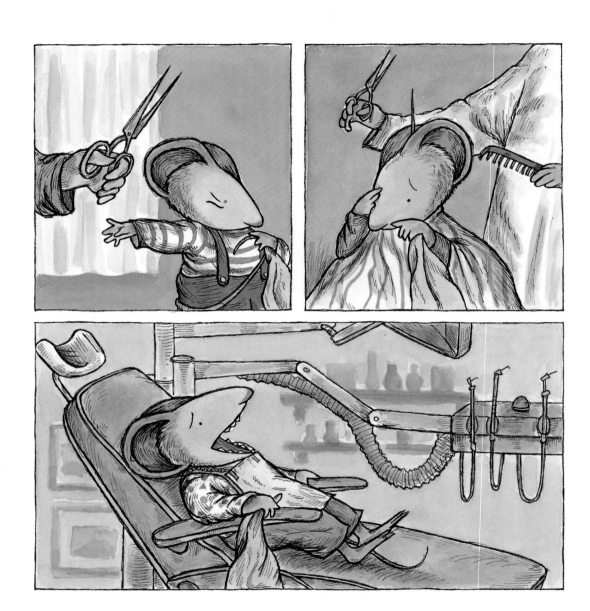

And Fuzzy was essential when it came to nail clippings

and haircuts and trips to the dentist.

"Can't be a baby forever," said Mrs. Tweezers.

"Haven't you heard of the vinegar trick?"

Owen's parents hadn't.

Mrs. Tweezers filled them in.

When Owen wasn't looking, his father dipped Owen's favourite corner of Fuzzy into a jar of vinegar.

Owen sniffed it and smelled it and sniffed it.

He picked a new favourite corner.

Then he rubbed the smelly corner all around his sandbox, buried it in the garden, and dug it up again.

"Good as new," said Owen.

Fuzzy wasn't very fuzzy anymore.

But Owen didn't mind.

He carried it.

And wore it.

And dragged it.

He sucked it.

And hugged it.

And twisted it.

"What are we going to do?" asked Owen's mother.

"School is starting soon," said Owen's father.

"Can't bring a blanket to school," said Mrs. Tweezers.

"Haven't you heard of saying no?"

Owen's parents hadn't.

Mrs. Tweezers filled them in.

"I *have* to bring Fuzzy to school," said Owen.

"No," said Owen's mother.

"No," said Owen's father.

Owen buried his face in Fuzzy.

He started to cry and would not stop.

"Don't worry," said Owen's mother.

"It'll be all right," said Owen's father.

And then suddenly Owen's mother said, "I have an idea!"

It was an absolutely wonderful, positively perfect,
especially terrific idea.

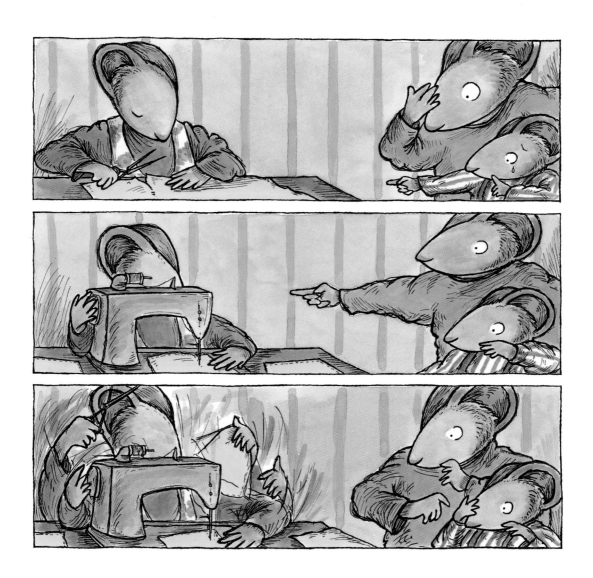

First she snipped.

And then she sewed.

Then she snipped again and sewed some more.

Snip, snip, snip.

Sew, sew, sew.

"Dry your eyes."

"Wipe your nose."

Hooray, hooray, hooray!

Now Owen carries one of his not-so-fuzzy handkerchiefs with him wherever he goes....

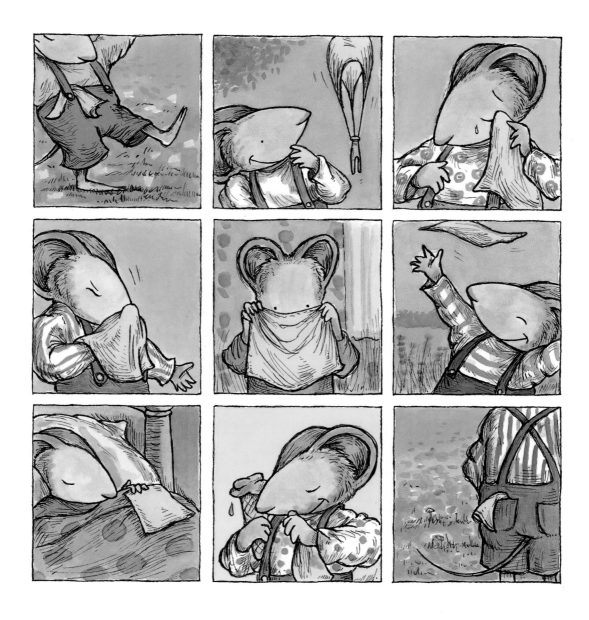

And Mrs. Tweezers doesn't say a thing.

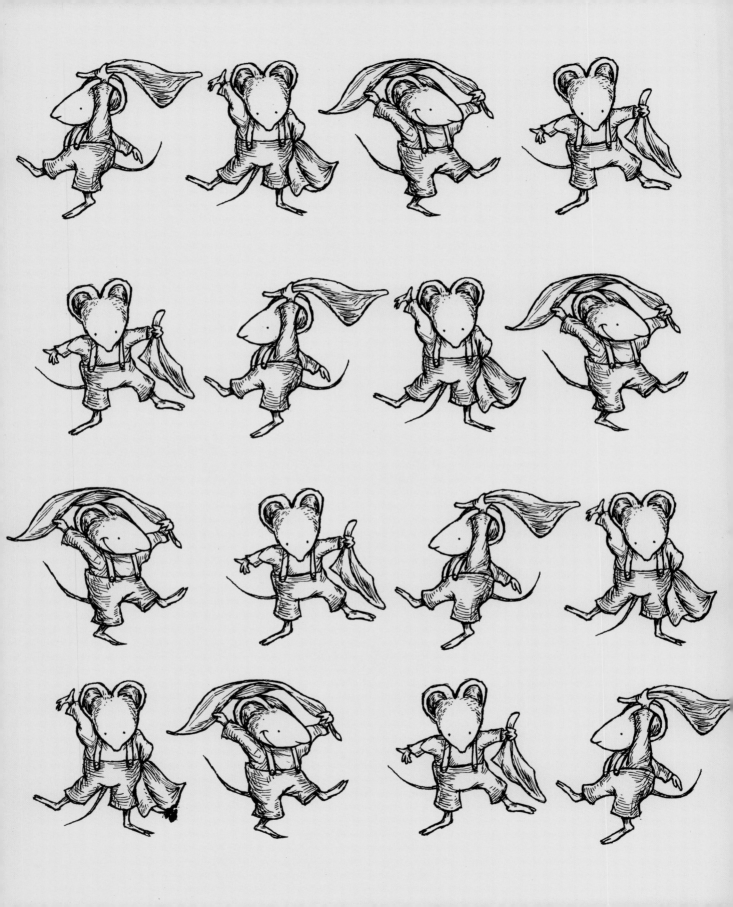

Some
bestselling Red Fox
picture books

THE BIG ALFIE AND ANNIE ROSE STORYBOOK
by Shirley Hughes
OLD BEAR
by Jane Hissey
OI! GET OFF OUR TRAIN
by John Burningham
DON'T DO THAT!
by Tony Ross
NOT NOW, BERNARD
by David McKee
ALL JOIN IN
by Quentin Blake
THE WHALES' SONG
by Gary Blythe and Dyan Sheldon
JESUS' CHRISTMAS PARTY
by Nicholas Allan
THE PATCHWORK CAT
by Nicola Bayley and William Mayne
WILLY AND HUGH
by Anthony Browne
THE WINTER HEDGEHOG
by Ann and Reg Cartwright
A DARK, DARK TALE
by Ruth Brown
HARRY, THE DIRTY DOG
by Gene Zion and Margaret Bloy Graham
DR XARGLE'S BOOK OF EARTHLETS
by Jeanne Willis and Tony Ross
WHERE'S THE BABY
by Pat Hutchins